BOY-MAN

Printed in Australia by Luke Weavell.
First Printing, 2016.

ISBN 978-0-9953704-1-8

www.lukeweavellwrites.com

For Donald,

My Taid.

Clem

'I'm pregnant,' Tilly said.

'*Ha,*' I said, and she furrowed her brow. I, too, was confused: I meant to say *huh*. I meant to express a long *huh*. I had no intention of *ha*, but it came out *ha*.

Tilly hesitated, as only one might after suffering a derisive laugh for impregnation.

'I'm sorry,' I said. 'I meant . . . It's just . . .'

'It's yours, Clem. You know that, right?'

'I–I know that.'

'Do you?'

'Yes.'

'Okay.'

'O*kay.*'

Tilly looked at me funny again. I knew I put the emphasis on the wrong syllable: I meant *o*kay as a peacekeeper might mean to say it. You know, like a police officer talking down a gunman. The kind of okay I should have accompanied with open palms. 'Open palms is an open person!' echoes the proverb of my mum. But I have not said *o*kay with open palms. I have said *okay* with closed fists, as a child might do when he grudgingly leaves his toys for the relatives when they come to visit.

Shit. That is what I am. I am a child who has no interest in his family.

No, that's awful – I am a child who appears to have no interest in his family.

No, that's ridiculous. It's like this: I am not ready for kids. Yes, that's it. I am twenty and not ready for kids. When they pull the baby from Tilly, the doctor will announce the sex and offer it to me and go, 'Here, Mr. Stevens, would you like to hold the baby?'

'Oh ho, no thank you,' I'll say, a casual wave to signal that I'm good.

Tilly frowned at me. 'You said okay funny,' she said.

'I did, yes,' I agreed. I glanced around the cafe. It's a Melbourne cafe, or at least an Eastern Suburb of Melbourne cafe, so there was a healthy mix of top-knot-and-neck-beard combos and flamboyant hand gestures. Sunlight warmed our table, and wind wafted from the open terrace. I sniffed and smelled coffee beans and sweet cakes and the perfume of the waitresses. Knowing my luck, the best-looking one would serve us.

And of course, I'm absolutely right.

'Hi, can I take your order?' the waitress asked and puffed out her chest to flaunt that she was '*Kihrstyn.*'

'A cappuccino, please,' Tilly said.

'Same,' I said. I prefer tea, but there's an art to it, there really is. People tell me there's an art to coffee making, but the only artistry in coffee I can appreciate is the pictures they make in the foam.

Kihrstyn scrawled down our order on a notepad, and I imagined a cursive so generic the police would find matches in a schoolgirls' cubicle.

'No worries,' *Kihrstyn* said. 'I'll be back in a sec.'

Kihrstyn turned around, and I looked away. Entirely because Tilly was there.

Tilly and I are funny. We were sweethearts in high school for years, dating from as far back as the time I used gel, through to the year I spent using wax, until finally I switched to my current styling product, neglect, and we broke up. I'd like to say my oomphless hair was what did us in, but that's coincidental. No, we were torn apart by expectation. How cliché, right? Not ours, mind you, others. Mums, dads, aunties, co-workers, gossipy hairdressers and eccentric people at the bus stop.

'Ah, oui, oui,' one jeweller said as I browsed her wares around the time of our fifth anniversary. I was eyeing a silver and aquamarine band. Simple, but Tilly liked teal and silver, so, sensible, right? 'Zees one,' the jeweller said, prying it out of the glass case with extra-long nails. 'Zees one is loverly.'

'Yes, it is,' I said.

'For Madame?'

'Yes.'

'Occasion?'

'Anniversary,' I said.

'Ah, magnifique. How long?'

'Five years.'

'Seelver?' The jeweller put a hand on her chest.

'Oh,' I said, cottoning on that I had offended tradition. Cottoning on that she had assumed too much. 'I'm not proposing.'

Suddenly, she raised a needle-thin eyebrow. 'Pur'aps you ought to.'

Damn Frenchy sowed the seeds of a sour anniversary. I could not get the thought out of my head. This girl, this girl who was more beautiful the more she dressed down, this girl who had been such a constant for so long that I had never even considered that maybe she wasn't to be.

It ruined me. I could not stop obsessing. How could I know if Tilly was the one? I didn't know what it would be like to date another girl who wasn't Tilly – would it be better, or worse? I realised I had no comparison. The hypotheticals killed me. What if she wasn't for me? What if she wasn't the one? What if I had another, concealed by the aura of Tilly?

My reason was doubt. Tilly's was need. 'You've been so distant. Tell me what's wrong. Tell me what you're thinking. Tell me what's on your mind.'

In the end, I did tell Tilly. I did, but not until after we were split, and even then it was a year after that. A boyfriend had come and gone by then. I figured Tilly could hear it; she deserved to know. I told her at a party, a mutual friend's house party that served as the template for all future high-school reunions. Beer pong championships co-existed with recycled philosophical discussions about everything and entirely nothing.

I told Tilly the truth. I told her I had doubts. I told her I had serious doubts. I breathed cider breaths right in her face and told her I had doubts about her. Now that calls for *ha*.

But, as it turned out, we got talking. I breathed at her, she breathed at me, we revisited old in-jokes and wandered our eyes over one another and thought the things drunk, high kids think about.

'Get inside me,' were her exact words twenty minutes later.

I don't remember, but I probably guffawed: I probably nervous-laughed the way the virginal nerds laugh in those college flicks. Get inside me. Guffaw.

'Well, gee, whizz! Okay!'

I'm not boasting here, mind you. It was the worst sex I've ever had.

'Is it in?' Tilly said.

'No, I've . . .'

'What?' she said, worried. 'Did you–'

'No, no. I'm soft.'

'Oh.'

'Yeah, I'm . . . wait a sec.'

'Do you want me to help?'

'No, no, it's okay, I'll . . .'

'You'll what?'

'Just gimme a sec . . . yep . . . yep, okay.'

'Okay, okay, okay,' she said, her breaths accelerating.

And here we are, a month later. Pregnant. Whoops.

The pill, as it turns out, has a 99% effectiveness rating at preventing pregnancy. Condoms have 98%. Without either, a few days before ovulation (primary baby-making time), the chances of pregnancy are about 30%.

You got to hand it to the kid: he or she went through a lot to get this far.

I came back to the cafe and looked Tilly up and down. She was wearing a white, floral shirt. I liked it. It was her. 'Why were you wearing a condom anyway?' Tilly said.

She would know if she really thought about it. A year had passed; I'm a cautious guy. 'I was drunk.'

'Right,' Tilly said. Her eyes flicked up. I smelled something sweet coming our way.

'Two cuppa-cinos,' chirped *Kihrstyn*. The mugs clattered down on the table. Coffee spilled down Tilly's mug; the waitress was careful with mine. 'Anything else?'

'No, thanks,' Tilly said and forced a smile. 'We're fine.'

Kihrstyn beamed, and then she walked away.

Tilly watched the waitress over my shoulder. She screwed her mouth, then looked back at me. 'What do we do?' Tilly said.

'I don't know,' I said, but I did. I knew Tilly. 'You want to keep it, don't you?'

'I didn't say that,' Tilly said. Her hands slipped beneath the table to touch her belly.

My mouth gaped a little. 'Abort it?'

'No,' Tilly said, and sighed. 'Look, I know we're not together, Clem.'

'We aren't?' I said, which hit in a way I'd not

really expected it to hit. I don't mean that I assumed we were together because we awkwardly made a baby together, I just mean it kind of disarmed me. It felt the same way arriving early at a not-so close friend's party feels: Where the hell do I stand? Do I get a drink? What are hands for?

'We . . . I don't know,' Tilly said. 'But this is us. This is our thing. It's not just my choice. It's ours. I want us to be on the same page. And I won't be one of those teen-mums who complains about their absentee baby daddies on Facebook.'

'They're the worst,' I said.

Tilly laughed. 'But I mean it. We're a team.'

The conversation was short: the baby stayed. We would go home and think on it. We'd tell the people we wanted to tell. Then we'd come back and figure this out.

That's what stuck with me after I watched her go to her car. Figure it out. I had a moment of clarity about what that meant. That meant diapers. That meant budgeting. That meant potty training. And if it didn't mean those things, it meant picking an orphanage. The right orphanage. Or a foster home, the right couple, the right would-be parents who were unlucky in the opposite way Tilly and I were unlucky. People we could trust. People who'd let us see the kid, and help us raise it and –

I realised there would be none of that. It would be raising the child on our own. It meant kindergarten, primary school, high school, uni, life. It meant the end goal was raising them into a well-adjusted person. And then a thought occurred. Tilly and I lived at our parents' homes, neither of us had degrees, and we were still the kind of people who had drunk sex at parties.

Holy shit I'm twenty and I'm gonna have a kid.

I needed to get my act together.

Clem

About thirty seconds after Tilly left the cafe, I got the sweats, bad. Stains darkened my underarms. My knees knocked together. I stammered another order to *Kihrstyn*, then bolted to the bathroom when she turned away. I crashed through the door, staggered to the sink, and spewed. Bile erupted from my lips and splattered in the basin. My eyes watered and my gut churned, then steadied. I stopped throwing up, let out a long sigh, and stood to face myself in the mirror. I was a certified wreck: not ten minutes after learning I'd made my ex-girlfriend pregnant, here I was, chucking. Just like Tilly will chuck, every morning, for the next few months.

'I've had the worst morning sickness,' I imagine Tilly saying.

'Yeah, me too,' I would reply.

And after her, the baby, and so the torch of vomiting will be passed, from me, to Tilly, to the baby. One big crappy family.

I wiped my mouth, elbow to wrist, and spat. My vomit started to stink out the grimy cafe bathroom, vile and acidic. All to myself, I shook my head, and muttered: 'I need to get my act together.'

First things first, I would quit my job. My crummy, peanuts-paying job. The one that taught me to check IDs, stack shelves, and nourish a slow but certain disdain for all living things: my job at a clearance store.

In my pocket, I had my letter of resignation, and so keen to quit was I, I actually skipped from my car to the cafe, and dared to dream that maybe, just *maybe*, this would be the best day of my life. I'd quit, get my girl back, and win the lottery – *Hallelujah, baby!*

Instead, I got an unwanted pregnancy, and I was no closer to quitting than I was to the end of my degree. Bum outta luck, as they say.

But I would quit, sure as Tilly was pregnant, I would quit today – but first I needed to stop shaking. I decided to call Cam and Johnno, my friends. Tilly said I should tell someone, and I wasn't about to tell my Mum or Dad or a sibling. Hell, I almost didn't wanna tell Cam and Johnno, but I had to tell someone. I had to talk about it. I had to stop the shakes. I called Cam and Johnno, but expected one or the other to say they were busy, Johnno house-locked by his blood alcohol reading, Cam just an introvert dick. Johnno was the first to arrive in his shiny-green Ute and his chrome wheels and his grumbly engine that he likens to a purr, but I think sounded way more like emphysema. Cam arrived on a Vespa. We sat around the same table where Tilly and I had sat. As soon as they arrived, I spilled everything so quickly I felt veins throb in my neck.

'*Hmm*,' Cam said and stirred his pinkie along the rim of his drink.

'Right?' I mimicked Cam's action. He looked nonchalant. I looked awkwardly sensual. I stopped fingering my mug, and drank it instead.

'Well,' Johnno said. 'What are ya gonna do?'

I sighed. 'Have it, I think.'

'Fair dinkum,' Johnno said, and his lip hairs bristled. I eyed him: he had thin, sinewy arms that poked knobbly from the sleeves of a Bintang singlet, stained with the sauces of pies past. He drank a coffee, since the cafe wasn't licensed, and I saw he had a lazily concealed lazy eye on the game on the television. Distractedly, Johnno didn't miss a beat. 'A little Clem runnin' around. Fair dinkum.'

'*Mmm.*' Cam stroked his hairless chin and jutted his lips. He wore a tweed jacket and half-spectacles. The only thing he lacked was a book at his side, perhaps Orwell, Steinbeck maybe.

'Have it, *mmm*,' Cam said. Even his *mmm* was mature, as if he ought to have been smoking a pipe while he said it. 'The stocks are plummeting, *mmm*, Pluto's now a dwarf planet, *mmm*.'

So, yes, I get that this is a strange meeting. Cam, as he is, will probably write as many novels in his life as he will finish caskets of brandy. Johnno takes a slab of VB to parties and refuses to share.

We are an unlikely three.

'Have it,' Cam said and clasped his hands. 'That's a very intelligent response.'

'MMM.' Whoops. I felt my eyebrows do a big arch, and I know *mmm* is Cam's alone. I cleared my throat, started again. 'Sorry, I mean . . . I don't feel intelligent. I feel quite dumb.'

And it was true. I did feel dumb. To an extent. To the extent that I didn't know what to do next. As soon as Tilly left the cafe, I ran to the bathroom and threw up. I'm sure intelligent adults don't do that.

'Dumb? How so?' Cam asked.

I thought. 'Well, maybe dumb is harsh.'

'Harsh, *mmm*.'

'Unprepared?'

'Unprepared, *ahh*.' That's where Cam would take his pipe and shake it gently, a gentlemanly nod to the epiphany. Cam had no pipe, so he made do with his finger. 'Then it's simple. How *do* you prepare?'

I think, not hard at all. 'I have to quit DRD.'

DRD was Down Right Deals. You know, that job I loathe? It's a clearance store. It's the worst.

'Quit?' Cam had his hand on his chest. 'Is that wise?'

'Bout bloody time, mate,' Johnno said.

I looked at the pair of them, from one to the other; from tweed-and-corduroy Cam to moulded-thongs Johnno.

'What?' Johnno said, but he said it without pronouncing the *h* or *t*. It was more grunt than word.

'Nothing, it's just . . .' I glanced at Cam, then at Johnno again.. 'Well, what do you guys talk about when I'm not present?'

Johnno did not even hesitate. 'Cricket,' he said.

'*Ah*,' I said. Mystery solved. 'Okay – seriously. Quit. Get a better job. Me. Today. Good idea, bad idea?'

'Call me clueless on the matter,' Cam said and leaned forward. 'But children, as I understand, come at an expense.'

'Money, right,' I said. 'I get that. So I get a better job. Better than DRD. Something that supports Tilly, the baby, and me. Good idea, bad idea?'

'Ripper idea,' Johnno said. 'But then . . .'

'But what?'

Johnno shrugged. 'What's the better job?'

Johnno once got a 10% on a maths exam. I now realise he was saving up all his 'right' for that one second. Goddammit. He's so right. He's so goddamn, bloody, damnably right. But . . . I really wanna quit.

Okay, okay, that was childish. I have to stop doing that. It's . . . Well, it's just . . . I really, *really* wanna quit.

I wish I didn't work at a clearance store, but no, I really, unfortunately work at a clearance store. If you're unfamiliar with what a clearance store is, I'll tell you. It's a place where all the stuff that isn't good enough for a regular supermarket ends up. It's where slightly out of date cereal ends up. It's where upside down labelled juice ends up. And it attracts a certain kind of crowd. No offence, certain type of crowd, but you are attracted to clearance stores. Fact.

I had a shift following my double-up coffee with Cam and Johnno, and I parked so I'm looking straight at the shopfront wedged between a Coles and a Woolworths. It's shitty, it's tiny, it's yellow, and even from here I can see the dust rise and settle with the inner shufflings of my colleagues and my customers. I walked in, and felt the sun hit my back like a smug younger sibling. 'Ha ha!' the sunlight chortled, or so I imagined it might. 'You have to work and cannot enjoy my loveliness! Now get on your knees and stack, you worm, *stack*!'

I spent the first hour of my shift stacking until I had a customer. Older gentlemen, wide of midriff, pungent of underarm.

'What's this price?' the old guy asked. Note he didn't ask *me*, he just asked the store and expected an answer. Customers never say 'Excuse me, how much is this?' No, they just wave something in the air, ask the store for a price, and expect some entity of the aisles to answer.

'A dollar,' I told the guy.

Then he looked at me, finally, and poked his tongue in his cheek. He dropped his weight on to one hip. This guy thought he got me. Customers always think they've got you. 'The ticket says eighty cents.'

'Are you sure?' I stacked more cans.

'Yep,' the guy said, and rustled his moustache.

I stopped stacking and I slapped my thighs and I stood. 'I'll just go check.'

'It *says* eighty,' he said.

'I'll just go check.'

He said nothing. His cheeks went red. I don't

19

know what he expected. *This is eighty cents!* No, it's a dollar. *Eighty cents!* You know what? Yeah, okay! It's eighty cents. And here – take this receipt. You will need it to get a refund tomorrow! And remember: be sure to bring the suspiciously licked-clean can for proof of purchase! You have a nice day now, okay? *Okay*, bye-bye now.

In aisle four I find the rest of the baked bean cans between canned spaghetti and canned tomatoes, and a ticket that says a dollar. Right next to this ticket there is another ticket that says eighty cents for porridge. I frown. A little because eighty cents for porridge is a bargain. Mostly because I'm about to witness some grade A bullshit. In fairness to the guy, there is a ticket that said eighty cents . . . even so.

I took the ticket and walked back to the first aisle. I caught the man scratching dangerously close to his nostril. 'It's a dollar,' I said.

'No,' the man said as he looked up.

'It is.' I handed the can back to him.

He shook his head. 'No.'

Oh boy. 'I'm afraid there was a ticket where there shouldn't have been.' I held up the eighty cents porridge bargain ticket for him to gawk at. 'There's porridge for eighty cents.'

'Well nah,' the guy said. 'That's false advertising.'

Ah huh. 'I'm sorry, just an honest mistake,' I said.

He smiled, held up the can again. 'So I can get it for eighty cents?'

'I'm sorry, but I can't give it to you for eighty cents,' I said.

'No,' the guy said. 'You have to give it to me for eighty cents.'

'I'm sorry?'

'It's the law,' the guy said.

Nope. Na'ah. Not true.

'I'm sorry,' I said. 'But I can't sell it to you at that price.'

'Then I don't want it.' The guy slammed the can on the nearest shelf, stormed past me, and left in a huff, muttering under his breath. I went back to stacking cans with a sigh. I wish I could've given it to him for less, I do. Or at least, I wish I had the option to give it to him for free. I can't, though. I did once, and got called into the manager's office.

My manager will be dead in less than six months. I don't know what from, but from something. She has a body mass index of sixty, drinks her liver black, and has two cigarettes per break in the dozen she has scattered across the day. I've never seen her cut herself, but I imagine her blood thick and pink with glucose.

'Look, Clem,' she once said after I gave an old woman leeway when she fell short five bucks. 'This is a business –' *cough, cough* '– and we have to run it as a –' *wheeze, cough* '– we can't –' *cough, splutter*; I wiped my cheek '– give away our stock to every –' *cough, chest pump*; blue veins pulsed on her head '– to everyone who comes in here.'

'Sorry, boss,' I said.

'Good,' she pulled out a cigarette. 'Go get me a coke, yeah?'

Stacking shelves, another customer approached me: a woman, bleach blonde hair and khaki pants. There's a sixty-five percent chance she'll ask to see my manager. 'How much is this?' She held up a bag of porridge. 'There was no price.'

'Eighty cents,' I said.

'Mm, no,' she purses her puffy lips. 'No ticket no price. That's the law, actually.'

I will go mad here.

Googly-eyed crazy if I stay.

I did the maths throughout the rest of my shift, making a mental shopping list: nappies cost fifteen bucks for a twenty pack. Baby formula twenty. Baby food ten. That's fine, that's cool: how much more would a baby need? *Toys*, my inner monologue answered back. *Lots of toys.* Ah, damn . . . I'm absolutely right. My kid'll want toys. That's okay, I can budget for toys. What else? *Clothes, you tit.* Yes, of course, I knew that. Clothes. Many clothes. But that's fine, because they'll last a while – *No, they won't. They'll last a month before the damn thing grows out of them.* Fine, so I'll get some more. Too late, of course, because the baby has grown again. Well, how about that? I guess I'll get two sizes up for next time. Oh what's that? The little one is teething and it's in agonising pain? Compacted tooth? Can infants even get those? I don't know and neither does my subconscious, but we both know we can't afford whatever the hell medical bills cost. And by Jove! In all that fluffing about, the child is now in prep, or would be if I'd paid the two grand deposit on my child's education. Well, screw it then, I'll home school them. No, I can't, I need to work to buy the now six-foot toddler more clothes. Two-grand it is, that's okay, we can manage as long as everything goes just right–

Car breaks down. Oil change. You'll have to pay it.

Then insurance.

Then registration.

On top of things, now.

No, you're not. Gas bill.

Paid.

Water bill.

Dammit. Alright, paid.

Electricity.

Bloody Hell, paid.

Rent.

Paid.

Speeding ticket.

What for?

Speeding.

Where?

On a road; now cough up, you miserable pleb.

Son of a . . . All right, paid. Now, can I please just have a moment's peace?

No. Not until Tilly no longer looks at you like some failure. Some moron who quits his job because he doesn't like it. Too hard, it's beneath me, it doesn't make me happy. When I tell her, what chance is there she'll rejoice? Slim, at best. None, realistically. So I'll find a better job, a better-paying job. A job I can tell other people about that I won't quickly interject with 'I also go to uni!'

I took a deep breath, clenched my fists and walked into my manager's office.

My manager stared at me blankly. She suckled a cigarette, and smoke wreathed around her head. 'Something you wanted to tell me, Clem?'

I crumpled my letter of resignation. 'No,' I said and binned the ball of paper. 'Nothing.'\|

Clem ☐

DRD got me four hundred dollars a week, so I made some calculations.

It was really not good. Like, no savings not good. Overtime not good. Extra overtime not good. Like, poverty-stricken, living on the dole, bumming change for the bus ride home not good.

And I saw it then: my life unfolded in a dismal, blurry swirl. I'd work an entry-level, minimum wage job for the rest of my life, marry out of necessity and loneliness, resent my family, hate my wife, pay out the money to Tilly's child while the creeping, ugly desire to end it all inched closer and closer until –

Okay, what the hell? No. *No.* People have kids all the time. Teenagers have kids all the time. I can do this. I can *do* this.

. . . Can't I?

My head hit the steering wheel the instant I got in my car. Today was . . . disappointing was too harsh, eventful too vague. Today was just not to plan. Yes, that's it: today was not to plan. I was supposed to quit my job, not keep it. I was supposed to win back Tilly, not get her pregnant. I know I should stop saying that. I should just accept it, right? I raised my head. Accept it. Yes. I am going to be a father!

Nope. My head dropped. Not yet. Maybe this was all a cruel joke: a nine month trick. Yeah, yeah, it was a joke – I turned twenty three months ago, which meant in nine months . . . *yes*, this was just a big joke, and I was the butt. Tilly will pretend to go into labour, scream and kick and cry, and then I'll say push, then the lights will go off, come back on, and confetti will rain on the faces of my friends and family, and the midwife I guess, and they'll all laugh and say 'Got you good!'

. . . I know, I know, that's ridiculous. Don't give me that look.

What am I doing? I lifted my head and grabbed the wheel. *Get a hold of yourself, Clem – you're gonna be a dad. Deal with it.* I tightened on the wheel. So I didn't quit my job. Big whoop. So I didn't get back with Tilly. Who cares? I had nine months before the baby came, and the rest of my life after that, to change those things. I had one off day. I'm going to be okay.

I turned the ignition, got the engine to grumble, and inched my way out onto the road. I went ten k's under the speed limit the whole way home.

Yes. Home. It's time to tell everybody.

Home was fine. There live Mum, Dad, my elder sister, my younger brother, and my fat dog. It's a brickwork, suburbanite kind of thing with a hedge *and* a white picket fence. I don't get it. Isn't the hedge the fence? I digress. I parked on the kerb outside my house, looked up the fenced hedge, and frowned, and then I stepped out into the cold night air and took a deep long sigh that chilled my lungs. Okay. Steady now, Clem. Just come clean. I shuffled up the driveway step by dragging step and kept both eyes on the house the whole time. It's one-storey, kind of small and there are no secrets. I breathed and opened the door into the hallway. By wild coincidence, Mum is there in a dressing gown with a cup of tea to her mouth. Her crowfeet eyes narrowed over the rim of her mug. 'Everything alright, darling?' she asked me.

'No.' I rubbed my neck.

'Did you quit?'

I shook my head.

'Oh,' she said. 'Never mind.'

'Yeah,' I said. 'And I got Tilly pregnant.'

Okay, stop. Stop for a second. Just stop what you're doing, and listen. *Listen* to me. Get a pen, get some paper, take a seat, and write this down: *Don't do the thing I did.*

28

You may add an exclamation point for emphasis.

'*Oh,*' my mum said and waved a tissue in the air like an amateur-theatre ghost, dabbing her eyes with the corner every second wail. She gushed; mascara ran in black, demonic streaks down her face. She wailed and moaned and caught her breath. Then she really unleashed. I mean, she really let me have it: 'I raised you better! Why weren't you more careful? You're not ready!'

I sat and held my knees and nodded. 'Yes, Mum. I know, Mum. Yes, I know, Mum.'

Straight after the very long, very intricate tirade Mum ripped out on me, she dabbed her eye once more and sighed. '*Ohhhh*!' she said again.

I almost reached for a tissue myself. Not because the news made me want to cry, (vomiting was quite enough emotional discharge for me) and not because Mum's rant hit me on any deep level, but because I had no idea what to think. The point is, Mum was right. I wasn't ready. I hadn't quit my job, and I hadn't finished my degree, and I hadn't made any waves to fix any of that. Sure, I'd only found out today, and most of that day was filled with explaining that beans were a full dollar to the can, ad nauseam, but the point remained: I was no closer to being prepared than I was when I first heard those two words come from Tilly's sweet lips.

I needed to get prepared, and my Mum was going to help me . . . That sounded better in my head.

'*Oh,* Clem! How *could* you be so careless?'

'I wasn't, Mum,' I said. 'Me and Tilly –'

'Tilly and I, dear,' Mum sniffed. 'Tilly and I.'

'Yes, okay: Tilly and I used protection.'

Mum wiped her eye again, pouting her lips. They glistened almost as much as her eyes. 'Well . . . I don't know, Clem.' She threw down her tissue. 'What the *hell* are you going to do?'

'I don't know, Mum.'

Mum waved at her eyes and sighed, then she sniffed long and hard, and turned to me. 'Did you say it was with Tilly?'

'Yes.'

'Oh good,' Mum said. 'That's something at least.'

'What does that mean?'

'Well,' Mum shrugged. 'She is the responsible one, Clem.'

'That's not true,' I said. 'I'm very responsible.'

'Of course you are, dear, just . . .' Mum said. 'Just not with things like this.'

'Babies?'

'Babies?' Mum's eyes widened. '*Not* twins!'

'No, I was being . . .' I put my hands way up, and

beckoned Mum back down into her seat. 'It's just the one, Mum. I swear.'

Talked down, Mum eased back into her chair and plonked her hands in her lap. 'It's just . . . you're not ready, Clem. Are you?'

Isn't that the truth? Mum was right. Johnno was right. It seemed the only person who had no answer was me. That's depressing. Do I laugh? Cry? Should I laugh myself into crying? No, no – another time. Perhaps in the morning, ironically, into a bowl of Cheerios. But not now. Now I had to give the answers.

'I can be,' I said.

'How?'

'First, get a better job,' I said. 'Then I get my degree, nail my studies, you know? All through that I find out everything I can about being a parent. I read, I talk to people who've had kids – everything and everyone.'

Mum nodded, and wiped her eye one last time. 'It will be hard.'

'I know,' I said.

She smiled. 'I'm just glad you and Tilly have sorted things out.'

'What do you mean?'

'Tilly and you, back together,' Mum beamed. 'It's nice.'

Yeah, about that . . .

We were supposed to, Mum. We were supposed to, but . . . I don't know. Tilly made it clear. Crystal clear. Made it abundantly, crystal clear that her and I, me and she, us together was no more.

You see it a hundred million times in all those rom-com movies where the guy calls the girl and spills his guts and that soft indie chart-topper plays in the background, first quietly, then explodes when the girl sobs real happy tears and you know, you just know things will be alright.

When I finish telling Mum everything, I dialled Tilly. It was nine o'clock, a full twelve hours since Tilly told me she was pregnant. It almost felt full circle, me telling her I loved her.

The phone answered. '*Hello*?' It was her.

'Tilly! Hi, it's me.'

'*Hey . . . uh, what's up?*'

'I've been thinking a lot about what you said.'

'*About getting me pregnant?*' she said.

'*That's . . . I mean, you should, right? I'd be worried if you hadn't.*'

'No, no, not that,' I said. 'Well, yes that, and not that. I meant the other thing you said. The thing about us not being together.'

'*Oh.*'

I imagined it now: Tilly lying in bed, a box of tissues at her side, her favourite movie on TV, the volume turned right down, and a box of comfort goodies – chocolates, nuggets, ice-cream, etcetera – while she looks solemnly toward the windows, just waiting for me to call, and when I do, she'll be biting her lip, hoping I'll say what she's been dying to hear me say for so long it's –

'*I'm with Jason, Clem.*'

The fantasy pops like a balloon and farts until all I'm left with is a deflated, soggy sack of a dream. 'Eh?' I said, because what else could I say?

'*Jason,*' Tilly said. '*My ex.*'

Then it hits me like . . . well, a *hit* – I mean, all hits hurt, right? This one was no different. Only it's more like a crushing blow. It *floored* me . . . the soggy balloon dream puffed right back up again, but this time Tilly was all smiles and laughter, and a tall, muscular man stood at the foot of her bed. She bit her finger, and he put his hand through his hair, and then slowly lowered onto the bed. I closed my eyes, but the vision stayed. The guy who stood before Tilly was Jason. Ex-boyfriend Jason. Ex-boyfriend gone and went and come again Jason.

'*I know that's not what you want to hear,*' Tilly

said. *'But after . . . well, after that night, I got thinking, and Jason, well, he . . . he was on my mind, a lot. I thought maybe I didn't give him a chance – because of how soon after you he was. And, well . . . we're giving it another shot.'*

My eyes stung. It was all just a twisting knife.

'I'm sorry, Clem. I am so sorry.'

I hung up the phone. Then I crawled into bed, pulled the covers over my head, and cried.

Clem

'C'mon, mate,' Johnno said. 'It's not *that* bad.'

'You're right,' I said, pacing on the spot. My fingers pulled and strained at my hair. My feet tacked on the sticky floor. 'It's so much worse.'

'Mate, don't get so worked up,' Johnno said. He munched another handful of popcorn. 'It's . . . you know, you'll get over it. It could be worse.'

'How could it be worse, Johnno?'

Johnno nodded at the full body poster on the satin wall. Harrison Ford grimaced beneath the brim of his hat. 'They could have re-casted.'

I scoffed, let go of my hair and walked toward the light in the foyer. The queue for the movie was thinner and shorter than when Johnno and I had first arrived together, dropped off by our mums as far away as possible, under our strict instructions. Being fifteen, our social policy was to hide, deny and omit any evidence of having, or previously having, a mum. I got Mum to park across the road. Johnno caught the bus.

'I liked the bit where the guy Tarzanned on the vines,' Johnno said.

I shook my head. 'Stop it.'

'And the bit where the spaceship took off.'

'I don't know who you are anymore.'

'*Oh* – and I loved it when the alien burned her head off.'

I stopped. Right in the middle of the foyer, I stopped, and started to pace on the spot. I listed every reason why Johnno's opinion was wrong, and, objectively, the movie failed. I went on, and on, and on some more.

'Clem,' Johnno said.

'And an Aussie as a Russian!' I grabbed Johnno by his scruff. 'An Aussie . . . as a *Russian*, Johnno. A Russian!'

'Don't care. Clem, look.' Johnno pointed over my shoulder. 'Isn't that that sheila you like?'

'Sheila? Really?'

'*Girl*, then. Still her, though.'

I turned around. Sure enough, at the end of the line, in a white floral shirt and her hair kept back with a band, was Matilda. My cheeks warmed and my chest tightened and I grabbed Johnno by the elbow.

'Clem – *ow* – you're hurting me.'

'It's her. It's *her*.'

'So talk to her, ya idiot.'

'I can't. She'll know I like her.'

'Yes, she will, dickhead. So do it.'

Matilda's gaze swept across the foyer; a gentle breeze graced her neck, and her hair quivered. Her eyes met mine, and for the briefest of moments, she smiled at me.

I think that was the happiest moment of my life.

'Go on, Clem,' Johnno said. 'What's the worst that could happen?'

I turned the photo of Tilly and I from the Debutant Ball face down on the bedside table and rolled over. Sunlight seared the back of my neck. Sweat steamed under my sheets. I might have a shower, I might not. If I did, I'd have to get up. I'd have to swing my legs over the mattress, touch down on the gritty wood floor, find my towel, undress –

Forget it. I pulled the sheets tighter.

I was fine. Just tired, was all. I had worked pretty hard, and I always have big sleep-ins after big days.

My phone rang. I wrung my pillow. Then I answered. 'Hello?'

There came a barrage of coughs on the other end. Dammit. '*Clem* –' cough, cough '– *can you* –' snort, spit '– *come in today, mate?*'

I opened my mouth. Or, more accurately, my top row of teeth rested on my bottom lip, and air sighed out in a long *'f'*. I nearly said it. Didn't, but I nearly did. My head spun and all I could think about was the whining cries of an unborn, unnamed child with its hands out. Then it swirled and it hurt and suddenly Tilly's shrill laughter split my ears, and the low rumble of thunder erupted from a third, ominous shadow that stepped forward to become tall, handsome, ex-boyfriend-now-boyfriend-again Jason. *How dare she! How dare she tell me we'd made a child and then cut me out for another guy.* A better guy, no doubt. One who self-improves and betters himself. *Well*, Jason, think you're so good with your nice clothes and your fancy sensitivity – I won't stand for it, dammit! I'll be better than you ever were. And I'll win. I'll win Tilly back. How?

Okay, well, first things first: I need to know how to handle an infant. Easy. I'll swing by the library after work, borrow all the books, then go home and compare notes with Mum and Dad. Easy said. Wonder if easy done. Probably not. But it's a start.

Second thing: I have to find a better job. Write up my resumé, then make it rain – fling every copy at every store, warehouse, supermarket, office, supplier and restaurant from here to Timbuktu. Probably not the city, though. Traffic makes me want to torch my car, and I don't like trains. I dunno, I just don't like them. Okay, so maybe it's not so much the trains as it is people and how I don't like smelling butter chicken unless I'm eating butter chicken. Just me.

Thirdly . . . Tilly.

By being a better person. Making something of myself. Becoming great. Maturing. Rising above. I'd fix my life; I'd be the father a child would boast about, an adult a child would aspire to be. That's how I'd do it. That's how I'd win.

But first, work. 'Okay.' Then, to the library!

Tilly rolled over to me. The blankets bundled between us. 'What's wrong, Clem?' she asked.

Our five year anniversary was coming up. I'd bought a silver and aquamarine ring. I knew she'd love it. And yet . . . I trembled a sigh, then gulped. 'Nothing.'

'Clem?'

'Nothing.' I rolled over.

Work was terrible. The law of inconsistent tickets equating to freebies came up again, and some punks stole some cruisers one bottle at a time – they took one from the shelf, unzipped their bag, went to the walk-in freezer, and came out empty handed (must've put the bottle down; as though). I didn't stop them. Go, kids, have fun. Wear protection. My manager ran me ragged. 'Go stack the shelves –' *cough* '– but man the register –' *cough, cough* '– the fridge is empty, stack it –' *splutter* '– and the register, keep on it –' my manager squeezed her chest '– restack the shelves –' *snort* '– and the fridge, Clem, refill the fridge!'

The line at the register got to a dozen impatient customers when she came to the front, an unlit cigarette in one hand, *Krispy Kremes* in the other, and said 'I'm popping out.'

'Here.' I handed Tilly the small box. She took it with her fingers – her gold bracelets jangled. A smirk eased across her face. She opened the box. The smirk stayed.

'Do you like it?' I said.

Tilly closed the box. 'Yeah,' she said. Then nodded. 'I'll wear it.'

I smiled.

Tilly swallowed, her smirk disappeared, and she reached into her bag and pulled out a rectangle wrapped in white paper. 'Here.' She gave it to me.

I tore through the paper. Harrison Ford glared at me from beneath his hat. *Kingdom of the Crystal Skull.* I tried to smile, but it came out a smirk.

'Do you like it?'

'Yeah,' I said. 'Yeah. It's good. I'll . . . I'll watch it.'

Tilly pursed her lips, and nodded. 'Right.'

Nine hours went by. Sweat ran like dark veins through the dust on my skin. I rubbed my eyes, rubbed my neck, exited the store into a hazy orange afternoon with a splitting headache and staggered to the library down the street. It was an old brick building, or at least old in that it had aged since the '70s. A thick layer of foliage covered the front lawn, and a plinth had been erected at the entrance in commemoration of a surgeon. Huh. Funny place to honour a surgeon. You'd think a hospital, but what do I know? I lurched inside, staggered to the parental care section, and piled the books in my arms. *Brain Rules for Babies; What to Expect When You're Expecting; Parenting for Dummies.* Up and up the pile towered. I heard montage music building in my mind. I'd read them all. I'd learn it all. I'd be the guy who stayed past closing and study all night on nothing but coffee, and then the librarian, a Morgan Freeman type, would sling his coat over his shoulder, smile, shake his head, and leave me to learn, knowing I'd be there in the morning, all tuckered out.

I plonked in a corner of the polished wood of the library, devoured the foreword of the thickest book, and stopped. Oh my god, how I stopped: like a Learner at a yellow light. *Babies are like eggs . . . they are, technically, from an egg . . . they can also be cracked, like an egg.* I closed the book and glared at the cover. There, smiling goofily, was the wiry-haired psychologist-author holding an egg: *Learning to Care with Eggs* . . . I don't what else I expected.

I slid the big book of eggs away from me and sighed. I couldn't read all this in a night. Who was I kidding? Nobody, that's who. I had worked nine hours, too, without a break – I could afford one sit down before I learned to be a parent. After all, I had eight months to win back Tilly and be a good dad and banish Jason back to the depths of Hell from whence he came. I had time.

I lugged the tower of baby books from the library back to my car, ashamedly, in two trips. Then I grabbed the wheel, put the key in the ignition, looked over my dashboard, and saw the cafe. I could go home, have a proper cup of tea . . . but for some reason I craved a cappuccino. Odd.

A coffee will do me good, I figured. Why else could I want one? *Listen to your body,* as they say.

'It's over, Clem.' Tilly wiped her eyes. She stood and pushed away from the wooden bench.

'Tilly. . .' I said. '*Matilda*.'

'I'm sorry.' Tilly pulled the ring from her middle finger and handed it to me. 'I can't.'

The cold metal band fell into my palm, so heavy I nearly fumbled. Tilly turned away. From behind, I saw her hands come to her face, and her whole body shuddered. I stood. I wanted to run to her. My knees trembled – pulled me towards her. My feet planted.

I just stood there and watched her go.

I got out of my car and shuffled to the cafe.

Inside, it's the same as it was. Beards and man-buns and low-cut tattered shirts that reveal rugged chest-hair, the smell of coffee beans and scented vanilla, and the table I had yesterday, empty. I took a seat there, and got out my phone, scrolling through the contacts. I could call someone. Have a chat. See what they're up to, but in the end I put it away.

'It's okay, let me,' I heard a voice say. Familiar. I looked up to see *Kihrstyn* approaching. A menu was in her hand. 'Hi!' she beamed. 'How can I help you?'

I felt my cheeks dimple. 'A cappuccino, please.'

Kihrstyn scrawled. 'Anything else?'

'No, thanks.'

'We're closing up soon,' *Kihrstyn* said. 'The cakes'll just get thrown out. Have your pick.'

I bit my lip.

Kihrstyn smiled. 'It might lift your spirits?'

When I looked up at *Kihrstyn,* I see her weight is on one leg, and her head is tilted to the side, and she's looking right at me. 'Okay,' I nodded.

'Yeah?' she said. 'What do you like?'

'Uh, cheesecake,' I said.

'Ooh – *good* choice,' she scrawled again. 'I'll be right back.'

I watched her go. Her ponytail swayed across her back, from side to side, with every step, a shimmer of brown and gold. Then she was gone, behind the counter. I sighed, and breathed again, and smelled perfume. It was nice . . . not that over-sweet stuff you get that stinks out the room, the gentle stuff. The stuff that turns your head. I shook mine though. *I have to focus: my job's crap, and the baby is eight months away, and I need to sort things out.*

Kihrstyn came back with cake and a cappuccino. She set them down before me and readjusted the skewed mug on the saucer. 'There you go.'

'Thanks,' I smiled.

'You're welcome,' she smiled back. Then she walked away.

I turned to inspect my coffee and free tea and beamed. I tried the cheesecake first. I took a bite. Sweet creamy heaven filled my mouth. Kihrstyn was right. I did feel much better.

Clem

Did you know only fifteen percent of mums have their water break before labour? I sure didn't – my only informant on pregnancy before Tilly and I fumbled up a child was Hollywood, and Hollywood had me thinking labour was a slip and slide.

I pushed back from my desk, trampled dirty clothes beneath the wheels of my chair, and sighed. I rolled my neck and glanced at the clock: one hour had passed. One hour of study. One hour of the physiological destruction of the female – you know what? Not important. I stood, and turned to my dirty room. Messy. Very messy. I saw that now, saw it in a way I had never seen it before. My work pants were on the bed, my shoes under the bed, bags everywhere, their contents spilling like innards from the zipper mouths. Rubbish, bowls, dirty cups, dust, dirt, stains – oh my word, this is revolting.

I spent an hour cleaning my room. Then I had a cuppa. And gave another hour.

When everything was where it ought to be, and the floors were clear and the cupboards neatened, I brush-clapped my hands. You know, like when anybody ever gets something done in a movie, or on TV? Then they say something like 'job well done' or 'that's the end of that chapter.' Well, that's how I clapped, and that's kind of what I thought, too. I mean, I'd accomplished *a lot*. I'd cleaned my room, I'd studied pregnancy, I'd . . . well, I still had my crummy job, but I chose to stay at my crummy job. That's mature, I think. Maturer than leaving. Is maturer a word? A mature person would probably know. Them or Google. First, I googled 'maturer a word', learned it wasn't, and kept listing what I'd accomplished the past month. I had cleaned my room, I had learned more about pregnancy, and I . . . had kept my job.

Oh . . .

I haven't done anything.

My butt hit the seat and my head hit the desk. I'm an idiot, aren't I? I'm one of those morons who posts all over Facebook how awesome their past year has been but doesn't mention specifics. 'Getting Tilly pregnant has opened so many doors I could never have imagined! I have learned so much! I'm so blessed. Can't wait for the next chapter of my life!' Plus hashtags. Eurgh. I am such a *peanut*. How could I have fooled myself into thinking anything had changed when everything was as it was before?*Well,* that's about to change. Fool me no more, *me* – I will get organised. I will find fulfilment, not employment. I will get a place, not tidy a room. I will *mature!* How?

First, money. Check. Second, knowledge. Check. Then . . .

I'm not sure, actually. I mean . . . the intent is there. The *will*, sure, the want to be better, to be wiser, more capable, but at my desk, in my neatened room in my parents' house, I don't know what step is next . . . if there is one at all.

How do you grow up?

The desk shook: my phone hummed on the wood. On the screen, I saw a number. Tilly's number, and her smiling face smooshed by me, kissing her. I watched it hum. I must never have changed her call picture. I guess, if she hadn't called me since we split, then I'd never have thought to look. I should change that. I watched the phone hum once, twice more, then I answered.

'Clem speaking,' *Clem speaking* – that's adult sounding, right? I played the 'I don't know who's speaking' voice, too. To demonstrate I don't care. That'll show her for choosing Jason.

'*Clem? It's Tilly.*'

'Oh *hi,* Tilly!' Now the 'I haven't seen you in ages' voice.

'Yeah. hi,' Tilly said. 'Listen, about the other night –'

'It's fine,' I said. This time without any voice. Just me. 'It's fine.'

'No, I'm not. . .' Tilly said. 'Look, just because Jason is in the picture . . . I don't want you to think that means I'm pushing you away, you know? You're still the father, okay? And . . . okay, I'm going to the clinic today, and I thought . . . I thought maybe you'd . . .'

Tilly paused. I bit my tongue. What, woman, what? Drive you? Watch your dogs? Alphabetise your bookshelf!? Just ask the damn favour!

'Come with me,' Tilly said. 'I'd like you to be there. Only if you want.'

Moments pass people sometimes. You know when you're just doing something, anything really, and your thoughts sway one way, and you are lost in a mindless wandering, fluidly shifting between nothing and – zoned out. That's it, I zoned out.

'Clem?'

'Yes,' I said. 'Yes, I do.'

'Okay,' Tilly said. 'I'll come pick you up.'

'Okay.' I said. I hung up, and pulled the phone from my ear to stare at the picture. Tilly and me, circa four year anniversary. Her cheeks were dimpled. I could see myself smirking, even with my lips on her cheek.

I locked my phone, and put it on the desk.

The car trip to the clinic was Hell.

I kept glancing at Tilly, inspecting her apparel. On her fingers, around her wrists, around her neck, in her ears, and just one spot on her nose, was gold jewellery. I searched over once more, and saw no silver. Maybe she was so devastated by our break up she switched. Then again, maybe she never liked silver.

Maybe *I* liked silver . . .

Tilly's car is clean, inside and out, so much so that even in those hazy afternoons where the sun glares through the window, you'd be hard pressed to find one speck of dust. Nothing. Nada. I don't know how she does it, and I don't know how I never noticed it before, but I noticed now. It made me rub my neck. Made me lean against the seatbelt. Made me want to tell Tilly to pull over. I almost did.

Ten minutes of silence passed before I turned to her, and despite my effort, my eyes fixated on her belly, now pressed up against an otherwise loose shirt. Tactically loose, I'm sure. I wondered if Tilly bought the shirt expressly for this trip, for her term in general, or if it was just lying around in a drawer between two tighter, floral numbers. If it was for the trip, she must've gone to the shops . . maybe asked for assistance. 'Excuse me,' she'd said and put one hand on her cheek to subliminally tell the clerk she was sorry to bother them, 'I'm sorry to bother you, but do you have anything that says 'silent car trip to clinic with ex-partner baby-daddy'? No? I'll try next door.'

Ex-partner baby-daddy. Was that my official title? Surely there was something shorter, less tiresome. I looked up from Tilly's baby bump, and caught her gaze. She looked away.

I sighed. 'What are we?'

'Oh, don't start, Clem.'

'I mean it.'

'Me too.'

'No, no I really mean it,' I said. 'If Jason is . . . who you *chose* –'

'*Chose*?' Tilly threw the wheel right. The car jolted. We swerved around the corner.

'Well, what would you call it, then?'

Tilly shook her head. 'I don't know.'

'Because it was a choice,' I said. 'And I drew short straw.'

'Yes, okay – *Christ*, yes it was a choice!' Tilly said. 'But not in the way *you* mean it.'

'. . . What do you mean?'

'Clem,' Tilly said. 'This isn't *Twilight*. If I wasn't with Jason, that doesn't mean I'd be with you.'

I remember the exact day I told Tilly I loved her. It was cold, and it was dark, well past dusk, and the rain slanted, so heavy, so hard. I draped a blanket around Tilly's shoulders and stoked the fire in a boyish attempt at romance. I remember the glint of light in Tilly's eyes. I remember the sweat on my palms. I remember the words jumbling in my mind. I remember the words spilling quietly from my lips. And worst of all, I remember her whispering back, 'I love you, too.'

I have no words.

I'd rather we leave it there for now . . .

'I'm sorry,' Tilly said.

No, that's it, Tilly.

'I didn't. . .'

Tilly, enough.

'It's not like that, Clem . . .'

We can't keep going.

'Clem?'

I already said my finishing line!

'Say something.'

'I understand,' I said.

Tilly gave me a very particular look. The kind of look a teacher gives a distracted student after they answer a question, or the kind of look I get from people when I tell them I'm not too hot on *Shawshank Redemption*. I mean, it's *pretty* good, but it's not – *distracted*. Clem, stay focused. Right. Anyway. Tilly's got eyes on me like I've said something she wasn't expecting, and to an extent, I feel like she's a mirror of my own surprise.

'You do?'

I bit my lip and scrunched my nose and gave it a real hard think. Sure, that night we confessed love was nice, but it was a long, long time ago. That's not who we were. I was the idiot who bought wrong gifts, I was the idiot who couldn't communicate my doubts and fears and let them ruin us. I was the idiot uncertain if we were meant to be, or stuck with one another, and I was the idiot wilfully content with either. And it was me, Clem, the idiot who thought drunkenly we had messed something up.

Slowly, I nodded. Once. 'Yes, I understand.'

Tilly's grip on the wheel loosened. Her shoulders lowered in the seat. Her lips parted, but she said nothing, and when I looked at her, all she did was smile.

'Hey, Tilly,' I said. 'Did you know only fifteen

percent of mums have their water break before labour?'

Tilly laughed. 'Don't change, Clem.'

'Too late,' I said.

Clem

The whole doctor's appointment kind of went by as a bit of a blur. Perhaps I had a lot on my mind, perhaps it was because hospitals smell like food and poo and I was stuck at a crossroads between disgust and intrigue, or perhaps it was the doctor himself. I mean, I totally zoned out, but I'm pretty sure the guy was gunning for a world record. *Most patient consults in one hour without the use of e-mail or phone.* When he burst through the door, he pointed right at Tilly. 'Tilly?'

Tilly nodded.

'Great. Baby's fine. Eat some nuts.' He turned to me. 'Get a haircut, son.'

And then he turned to leave. In just the nick of time, I snapped out of it. 'Wait!' I said. 'I have a question.'

The doctor stopped. 'I'm very busy, son – but here's the run-down. Get a bowl, put it on your head and just cut. Takes five minutes.' He turned to leave again.

'No, no, not that,' I said. 'I have some concerns.'

The doctor sighed. Then he turned. 'Go on.'

I smiled. 'Okay, so, you know how they say the body changes during pregnancy?' I said. The doctor's head went limp. He rolled his neck, his eyes, both shoulders, and thrashed his tongue. I *think* . . . he may have been annoyed. Hard to tell. I went on. 'Right, okay, so my concern is more to do with Tilly than myself, but I was reading the other day about a thing called *post-naval depression.'*

'Natal,' the doctor said. 'She's not a sailor.'

'Natal, sorry,' I said. 'So I was wondering, is there any way we could . . . bypass the chance of that kind of thing? You know, avoid it before it happens?'

'Look.' The doctor folded his arms. 'I've been through this with Tilly here. The best thing to do for Tilly is for her to monitor how she's feeling, and be vocal with me if she has any concerns. Okay?'

I nodded. 'Okay.'

'The take-away from today should be that your baby's fine.' The doctor smiled for the first time. 'Have a good day.' Then he left the room.

I grinned. That made me feel better. I'd been studying all this stuff like a madman in recent weeks. I was learning more and more every day, and every day I was more and more prepared to care for Tilly and the baby. I was ready. I turned to look at Tilly. Her lips were pursed.

'What?' I said.

Tilly grabbed her bag and shook her head. Her

lips relaxed, and she stood. 'Nothing, Clem. It's fine.'

'What?' I said. 'Seriously, what did I do?'

'Nothing.'

What the hell? I mean, I've heard mood swings can be prevalent in young mums. Hormones, and the like. But c'mon. She literally just heard her baby is fine, and for no reason, she's annoyed with me? It's like the doctor – what is it with me today? The walk back from the doctor's office, through the grim reception, to the car was awkwardly, aggressively silent. On both our parts.

In Tilly's car, when the doors clicked shut, I turned to her.

'What did I do wrong?'

Tilly sighed, then she looked at me. She sighed, composed herself. Uh-oh. Oh, boy. *Composed.* That's not good news . . . I don't want to generalise here, but in my experience – and I'll admit that extends about as far as Tilly, Mum and one or two teachers from high school – women compose themselves to destroy you. With critical facts. It's like a courtroom drama where they're the District Attorney prosecution and you're a fresh-faced, down-on-your-luck newbie who took the case the night before. You have a defense, but you kind of hope you get through it all based on your unthreatening obliviousness and some empathy on their part. Add a little neck-shrinking, maybe some high-pitched replies . . . not an admirable move, but you're a cornered animal at this point.

Tilly breathed in. Breathed out, and then . . .

'I know you're trying to be supportive,' she said. 'But there are some things that aren't your business.'

It's quiet in the car. And yeah, my head does the shrinky thing. 'What do you mean?'

'Post-natal depression?' Tilly said. 'Come on, Clem, you can't . . . I mean, that's not your *thing*.'

'I'm being supportive!'

'You were being *protective*!' Tilly said.

'What's the difference?' I said. 'Support, protect – same thing.'

'No, not same thing,' Tilly said. 'Support is coming with me to see the doctor. Protect is planning for the worst possible outcomes. It's like some . . . *bizarre* way for you to play hero.'

Head shrink. 'I'm not playing hero.'

'Are too!'

High-pitched. 'Am *not*!'

'*Clem*!' Tilly shouted. Her hand sliced through the air like a knife. My neck tightened. She breathed in again. 'Clem, I don't . . . I'm a grown woman. I don't need you to protect me. Okay?'

'. . . Okay.'

So Tilly is definitely going through some hormone imbalances.

I don't blame her. I've read a lot about it all. Mood swings, strange cravings, even aggressive outbursts. Not her fault. I just have to keep doing what I'm doing, you know? And that means being supportive and fixing her problems.

Tilly dropped me off home, quiet, but she still managed to mutter a 'Thank you for coming' and drove off. I felt good. Really good. For the first time in a long time, fantastically good. My baby was healthy – which made me feel all tingly. I guess that meant I'd finally accepted it. That was nice, too. On top of that, Tilly was letting me get involved. Letting me help. That's more than can be said for Jason. Where was he? Probably at home, like a chump, not reading up on pregnancy, or being a father – that's not supportive.

I walked straight inside, feeling good. Feeling great. The house was clean and smelled like the early simmering of dinner, and when I strode to the kitchen, following my nose, Mum was at the stove, humming.

'Hi, Mum!'

'Clem – you're in a good mood.'

'I am.' I took a seat on a stool behind the bench. 'Very good mood. Saw the doctor; he said the baby was healthy.'

'Oh, *Clem*, that is good news.'

'Yeah,' I guffawed, then I stopped. Something panged in my neck.

Mum glanced at me, but kept stirring the pan. 'Darling, what is it?'

I rubbed my neck. 'Well, Tilly and I . . . we fought. In the car.' I screwed up my nose. 'Twice. There and back. And then a third time in drive through.'

'Oh, that's no good,' Mum said. 'What about?'

'Well, I wanted nuggets, but she wasn't feeling –'

'Clem, no,' Mum said. 'I meant the real fights.'

'Oh . . . Yeah, right,' I said. 'Well . . . the first was about us. Like as a couple.'

'Oh *no*.'

'No, no, it's all right,' I said. 'She just said she doesn't want to be with me.'

Mum stepped away from the stove, arms outstretched at me. '*Oh* Clem, come here!'

'No, Mum, it was good,' I said. 'It was . . . That's not the bad part.'

Mum drew in her arms and twiddled her digits.

'It's not?'

'No.' I shook my head. 'The bad part is Tilly said I was being protective and not supportive.'

And then I told Mum all about the appointment, about the clinic, the doctor, the fight, and Tilly. I left out the Macca's run, but yeah, okay, not important. After all had been recounted and remembered, Mum and I were on the couch, sipping a fresh cup of tea, and suddenly I realised it had all blurred by me again. When I finished, I looked back over my shoulder at the kitchen. 'What happened to dinner?'

'*Clem*,' Mum said.

I looked back. 'Yeah?'

'I think,' Mum said and took a big gulp of tea. *Oh*, that irks me. Have you ever noticed people who do that? They start talking then they drink or take a bite of something so they have to stop, or worse, *talk* as they *chew?* Barbaric. It's like they're pausing for dramatic effect: '*Do you know the meaning of life? I'll tell you, right after I finish going to town on this turkey sub.*' Anyway, Mum took a sip, leaving me enough time for that segue, and then she breathed. Uh oh . . .

'I think Tilly has a point.'

'Mum, *no*, you're supposed to be on my side.'

'There are no sides, Clem,' she said. 'But Tilly has a point. You're obsessing over the bad things that *could* happen, but you're not enjoying the wondrous thing that *is* happening.'

'I am.' I shrunk my neck. 'I totally am! It's just I'm just preparing for anything that goes wrong. I think that's quite mature.'

Mum screwed up her face. 'I . . . *sort* of see what you're saying.'

'Thank you.'

'But being prepared for bad things is contextual,' Mum said. 'And you can't plan for every single bad thing that could possibly happen, Clem. What if tomorrow you were in a car accident? How do you prepare for that?'

'That reminds me.' I reached for my phone. 'Tilly doesn't have ambulance coverage.'

'Clem, that's not . . .' Mum began. 'Okay, yes, you should tell her that. But that's entirely different from planning for anything bad, like depression, or bankruptcy, or god forbid, something worse.'

I put my phone down. 'How?'

Mum sighed, had another sip of tea, and composed herself again. 'You want to support Tilly, yes?'

I nodded, my neck growing with each enthusiastic nod.

'Well,' Mum said. 'Be there for her.'

I frowned. 'Be there?'

'Yes,' Mum said. 'Bad things are going to happen, Clem, whether you're ready or not. Stop them, if you can, but for the things you can't, the things that hurt the people you love, it's often more than enough to just be there. To listen, to help, if they ask you to. That's support, Clem. I think that's what Tilly wants from you.'

I swallowed. My eyes pinched a bit. Stung, even. I bit my tongue so nothing poured out of them.

'Okay, now.' Mum finished her drink. It still bothered me. 'Now, let's finish that stir fry, huh?'

Mum leapt from the couch, stretched her legs, and walked back to the kitchen. I stayed on the couch, closed my eyes, and breathed. Then I picked up my phone, and tapped to find Tilly's name. I started typing:

I'm sorry about today. I just wanted you to know I'm here for you.

Tilly replied instantly:
Thank you, Clem.
I know now :)

You're welcome :)

:)

*That doctor was something
though, huh?*

Who.is this?

Is this a joke?

Who is this?????

Clem? The father of your future child?

Jason got my phone!

Oh okay

Clem I never told him!!!!

Is this a joke?!

*He just got took my car.
I'm freaking out!*

*It's okay, it's okay, I'm here for you.
Where do you think he might go?*

Clem your address is
in my GPS!

Oh no.

Oh god no.

Oh please god no.

Tilly

Oh god what have I done? Oh god oh god oh god – I forgot to tell my boyfriend about my baby with my ex-boyfriend. Not forgot. I'm not . . . *forgetful*, I just . . . Okay, look, have you ever had a kid? It's not an everyday thing. It's not *light* conversation. 'Hey, babe, what did you get up to?' You see where I'm coming from?

Okay, okay – calm yourself, Tilly. Remember your exercises. Breathe in the positive, breathe out the negative. In, out . . . In, out . . . Okay, now what's the problem? Well, for a start, Jason is pissed. Not great, but manageable. What else? He knows about Clem. That's where it gets problematic . . . because Jason now knows where Clem lives.

Oh *god*, what have I done? I swiped up my phone and punched Clem's number. He had to be warned, properly. Not a rushed text. The line began to ring, and then it picked up.

'*Hello*?' Clem's voice said.

'Clem! Oh my god, I'm so sorry I –'

'*Hello*?'

'Yes, hello, Clem. Look, Jason's pissed –'

'*Yeah, hi, this is a recording. I'm not available.*

Leave a message after the tone. Bye!'

The phone toned.

'ARE YOU KIDDING ME RIGHT NOW CLEM YOU STUPID FU –'

I stopped myself and hung up. Ever since the baby . . . Okay, this sounds stupid, but . . . I've tried to cut out swearing. You know, because of the vibes? It's stupid, I know, but I figure . . . if you play classical music to make your baby smart, then maybe swearing has an effect too. Is that stupid? I don't know, sometimes I think . . . I don't know what I think.

I tried to call Clem four more times, and left four more appropriate messages. Then I tossed my phone aside and lugged myself to the lounge room, step by disgruntled step. I'm so heavy. Really, seriously, this kid is so heavy, I feel like I'm simultaneously putting on weight whilst getting leaner. *Tilly* – not helping!

I hobbled to the chair, pivoted, and eased into the couch. I shouldn't complain. It's obviously not as bad as I thought, since Jason never noticed. That said, Jason and I haven't *really* – you don't need to know that. All that matters is Jason never noticed, and maybe I'm making a mountain out of . . . well, a baby bump.

Settled in my chair, I took another deep breath. What do I do? Clem's not answering, Jason is on his way.

And there's no way he'll listen to me just yet. Hell, maybe ever again. He got so furious: his eyes bulged, his knuckles whitened. Then he stormed out the door and bolted for my car. *Mine*, because he doesn't have one. Dammit. I'm stuck here in this house. Clem won't answer. But . . . maybe his family? Of course! I grabbed my phone and dialled Clem's mum.

The phone rang twice. Then, '*Hello?'*

'Kerry? It's Tilly, I . . . This isn't a recording, is it?'

'*No, Tilly, it's not. What's up?'*

I always found it strange hearing adults say phrases like that: *what's up, cool, awesome.* Seems dorky. I ran a hand over my belly, and I looked down. I guess one day, that little bubba is going to say the same thing about me. About Clem . . . Huh, that's funny.

'I'm sorry to bother you,' I said. 'It's just . . . Something's wrong, and I'm worried. Is Clem there?'

'*No, he's not here.'*

'Please, Kerry. I know Clem is probably upset with me, and he has every right to be, but I need to –'

'*No, dear, I mean Clem's not here. He left,'* Kerry said. '*What's going on?'*

Gone?

It never occurred that Clem might not be there. I thought . . . well, I didn't think he'd run. But where would he run to? Not work, not my house. . . where the hell would he go? Over the phone, I stammered: I couldn't think of the words fast enough, and I froze like an anchor without a prompter.

'*Tilly?*'

'I'm sorry, Kerry . . . I just didn't expect him not to be there.'

'*Yes, well, neither did I.*'

I stammered again. What do I say? 'Sorry, Clem's mum, but I didn't tell my boyfriend I'm pregnant with your son's baby and it looks like we better start placing bets'? Goddammit! What the hell am I going to do? They're going to kill each other! Jason with his bare hands, and Clem . . . Maybe with some lucky hits. All right, so maybe Jason's gonna be fine, but Clem could be done for this world. Tomorrow I could be planning his open casket, and the bouquets, and next week I'll dab my cheek while behind me his mother wails, his father trembles, and that waitress from the cafe . . . wait, what's she doing there? She doesn't know him! All she did was give him the eye a couple of times while he gave it back. That doesn't –

'Kerry, I might know where he is!'

I was a mixed bag of bubbling emotions in the car with Clem's mum. Awkward obviously, because, well, I got picked up by my ex's mum and that ranks highly on the scale for uncomfortable car rides, up there with school teachers and old friends whose lives have turned to shit . . . past experience. Terrified because Jason is on the hunt. Worried because Clem's the hunted. Doubly worried because Clem's hideout is the cafe. And triply worried because he might not be at the cafe. And finally hungry for pickles from the jar. I don't know if that's cravings. It's probably just cravings. I can't be sure of what's me and what's not anymore.

'Tilly, where is it?'

'Just around the corner.'

Kerry turned the wheel. I lurched, straightened, peered over the dashboard, across the carpark, through the open terrace to the cafe, through the denizens, and finally to Clem's favourite spot.

Clem was there.

Across from him sat Jason.

Clem

One hour earlier. . .

When I was much younger – primary school young, even – I ran the worst time in the hundred metre dash out of my entire class. Granted, two-thirds of my class ran district, and some were edging on state level, but none of that mattered to my teacher, Mr. Dunston, who tried with all his might to find what motivated me, and get me to run just that fraction faster to take a decimal off his average. Reflecting on that today has made me realise two things: one, that Mr. Dunston was a teacher for the wrong reasons, and two, that he was right about me lacking motivation. Today, I learned what that motivation was.

As soon as I read Tilly's message, I could have made state. Mum barely had a chance to stop me, and mustered only a rushed shout. I didn't make it out. I zoomed to my car, yanked open the door and jumped in so quickly I nearly landed in the passenger seat. I had to get out of there. I had to move. Jason already had thirty seconds on me. Thirty full seconds – that can be whole *days* in a high-octane thriller movie. I started the car, grumbled out of the driveway, and turned left. I didn't know where I'd go. I just knew I had to leave. The wheel was slick with my sweat. My heart nearly did its best *Alien* impression. I've never met Jason, but I've seen pictures of the guy – even pictures next to Tilly. Suffice it to say, Jason is taller than me. He's also wider. Not in the guts, mind you, in the shoulders. And the arms, and the neck, and the chest. So . . . you know, you do the math.

I turned the corner. My shoulder hit the door. The car behind me honked. I straightened, wiped my eyes. Where would I go? Where was *safe*? Work? Ha. No. Tilly's? It'd be the last place he'd expect – am I insane? No. Where? *Where?* And then it hit me. Funny in those instances of panic you can't think straight . . . I have friends, remember?

I turned another corner and drove to Cam's.

Cam's house is not like you'd expect . . . Well, I don't know what you expected, but it certainly wasn't what I expected when I first saw it all those years ago. For a guy who says *mmm* precisely like he'd fit right in among a circle of scholars, scientists and academics and might be able to add something to the conversation, he lives on a street known for its asbestos and graffiti. And I say graffiti with the negative inflection, as in, penis tags and dribbly print kind of graffiti. The stuff you're happy is buried under white paint. The stuff that turns you into a six-thirty news eye-witness when it returns: *I think it's a bloody disgrace! So disrespectful. Awful, just awful.*

I parked in the street in a one-hour zone, then I hurried to the wire fence, wrestled with the rusty latch, navigated the overgrown lawn to the front door and pressed the doorbell. *Ding, ding.* From inside there came muffled footsteps, then a shape moved behind the frosted glass. 'Whoever could that be?' came Cam's voice. The door swung open, and there he stood . . . in trackies.

'Ah, Clem! What a pleasant surprise. How are you?' Cam said.

'. . . What on earth are you wearing?'

'These old things?' Cam raised his leg like we were talking about his shoes. 'These are my recreationals. Come on inside. Johnathan is here.'

I followed Cam into his house, closing the door with my foot. 'Johnno's here?'

'Yeah,' Cam said, then quickly, 'I mean to say . . . *mmm,* the very same.'

Cam brought me through his 70's style kitchen, lounge and hall to his 'rumpus'. Sure enough, across from the PlayStation and the big-screen TV, was Johnno. The controller was to the side.

'Johnathan,' Cam said. 'Clem has joined us.'

'G'day, mate!' Johnno leapt to his feet. 'How are ya? Haven't heard from you in ages.'

I sat beside Johnno and laid it all out. Everything. From the study to the doctor's appointment and now with Jason. When I finished, breathing in slowly, Cam's thumbs were going mad on the controller, and enemies were dropping like deadweights on the TV. Johnno leaned back and sighed. He had a single finger on his lip . . . I was very confused.

'Cam, why are you playing a game?'

Cam glanced at me, then back to the screen. 'Pardon?'

'You like cricket, and port and leather-bound books,' I said. 'You don't like games.'

'On the contrary,' Cam said. 'I quite enjoy them.'

'No, no,' I said. 'No, Johnno likes games.'

'I don't like games,' Johnno said. 'I get bored.'

I frowned. 'Really?'

'Well, yeah, but . . .' Johnno said. 'Look, let's stay focused. Listen, as I see it, you're running from your problems.'

Hey, fella, you're supposed to be my support base. I shook my head.

'You kinda are,' Johnno said.

'I am not.'

Johnno sighed. 'Cam?'

'Indeed,' Cam said, then muttered, '*terrorist scum.*'

I got to my feet. 'Well . . . that's easy for you to say.'

'Yeah, but it's true,' Johnno said. 'What are you gonna do, run and run for the rest of your life till you or Jason drop dead?'

'No,' I said. 'I just . . .'

Johnno frowned. 'Just what?'

I bit my lip. 'I just need time, you know? Time to . . .'

'To what?'

My fists clenched.

'To what, Clem?'

'TO BE *READY*!'

Johnno stepped back. 'Whoa guy.' He raised his hands. 'Ease up.'

I shook. My nails dug into my palms my fists were so tight. I breathed heavy and fast. Johnno stepped back again. Cam paused his game and sunk into the couch, picking his nails. I scowled at the pair of them, these friends of mine, and they slunk back. I was here all of ten minutes, and already I turned to leave.

I drove to the cafe. I didn't know where else to go. I had no idea where I could go. I don't know why, but I like it here. Everything about it should make me feel uneasy. Here is where I learned I made Tilly pregnant. Here is where I realised I couldn't leave the job that drove me insane. And here now is where I sat afraid for my life that at any moment an angry man was about to kick my head in. I should hate it there, but . . . I don't know, I like the vibe. I feel comfy.

I sat down at my usual seat, and looked around. I didn't see . . . Well, not that I was looking . . . There were no waitresses I recognised, is all. And that . . . well, yeah. I grabbed the menu and flipped through the menu. I'd get a tea. Sure, why not. They probably won't use tea leaves, but live a little. Eventually, a waitress walked up to my table. She looked me over once, then smirked. 'What can I get for you?'

'Tea, please,' I said.

'Of course,' she said, then turned back.
'There's . . . a *delay* with the tea. I hope that's alright.'

'Yeah, that's fine,' I said. 'How long exactly?'

'Should be ready at four-thirty,' she said, then

left. That was weird. I unlocked my phone. It was four-fifteen now. I pocketed my phone again. Very weird. I leaned up against the window and stared outside. White clouds started to darken and spread over the blue. Great. Terrific. I zipped up my jacket as the waitresses closed the doors to the terrace, and the second the latch clicked, it started to pour. Rain streaked the windows. Puddles rippled on the footpaths. Steam wafted from my lips. I checked the time again. Four-sixteen. Dammit. This was no good. Not the tea part, I meant . . . all of it. It was cold here. I was afraid to go home. Furious my friends weren't more supportive. Now I was here and I couldn't go anywhere because if I did they'd find me and if they found me then . . .

I sighed, and drew in a lungful of cold air, the same way I might if I were composing myself for something. Something like messaging Jason to meet me at the cafe. At four-twenty-one, my phone buzzed with his reply.

Ok, it read.

Clem

I have come to the realisation, rather suddenly I might add, that I am not smart.

How did I arrive at this epiphany? Well, interestingly, it was an accumulation of mistakes that led me to this conclusion. Firstly, the whole *Tilly-baby* thing. Secondly, the whole Jason wanting to kill me about the *Tilly-baby-thing* thing. And thirdly, the whole messaging Jason to come meet me about the whole *Tilly-baby-thing* thing.

Oh yes . . . I am an idiot.

I started sweating immediately after I realised what an absolute dip-shit I had been. My hands went clammy, the shirt on my back started to cling to my soaking skin – outside the storm thundered on. That's the worst: when it's freezing, but you're sweating like a pig. I've never been anywhere tropical, but I imagine it's kind of similar to having a panic attack in the rain.

I panned my gaze across the cafe. The waiters and waitresses cleared tables, took orders, closed off the gazebo, and cranked the heater. I looked at the time: it was four-twenty-one. That moment a bell went off from the door. Oh God help me it's him –I wheeled in my seat and . . .

Khirstyn, the waitress, walked through the door, took off her jacket, and went behind the counter. She veered for two other waitresses, and they exchanged some jolly hellos. Then one of them pointed at me. I tore my eyes away and strained to hold back the torrent of nervousness I felt dampening my forehead. Come on, Clem. Hold, you son of a gun, *hold*.

Footsteps thumped from behind me – Khirstyn was coming closer. I knew it. I could smell her perfume. Oh dear. Okay, okay, just be cool. I turned to watch her approach. Khirstyn was nowhere to be seen. Jason stopped beside my table.

'Clem,' Jason said in a voice like a lumberjack crossed with a senior lawyer who keeps whiskey in crystal bottles in his high-rise office.

'J–Jason,' I said. My voice cracked.

Jason nodded. His black hair was wet. Strands ran down as low as his chiselled cheekbones. He flexed his hand. 'Can I sit?'

'Ah – yep, ah huh,' I said.

Jason thumped to his seat and sat with a heavy thud. He cleared his throat, sniffed and wiped his nose.

'Um. . .' I began. 'Thanks for coming?'

'Did you sleep with Tilly?' Jason said.

I swallowed. Jason was right there in front of me. And I was there – I was right there opposite him. I gulped and forced myself to speak. 'Yes,' I said.

Jason's mouth widened, and he let out a single sob, as if he'd been holding his breath. And then I saw his eyes. His glistening, bloodshot eyes. He sniffled, clenched his teeth, and took a deep breath. 'When?'

My skin dried, and prickled. 'At a party . . .'

Jason leaned back, and shoved his palms into his eyes. 'I knew it, I *knew* it,' he said.

I leaned back, too, slightly out of breath. I felt weird . . . not nervous, not uneasy, not panicked. My heart kind of beat along like normal, no skips. My chest didn't hurt, my hands didn't clench. I just had nothing to say.

Jason regained himself, bleary-eyed, sniffling. 'So . . .' Jason said. He laughed, stopped, and wiped a tear that trickled down his angled cheek. 'There's a baby, *huh*?'

My head just sank. So low, I looked at my feet. 'Clem?'

'Yes,' I spoke to my shoes, watching my toes wriggle under the laces. 'There's a baby.'

Jason made a blubbery sound.

I looked back up at the man opposite me. This

man who was trembling just trying not to cry. This man who was hunched over, as if everything inside hurt. This man who was in agony . . . because of me. Because of something I had done. 'Jason. . . I'm so sorry.'

Jason took a shaky breath, and steadied. 'I know it's not . . . It's no one's fault, you know?'

Ah ha – and there's the skipped heartbeat. '*Jason?*' I said.

'What?'

'Nothing,' I said. 'It's just . . . I thought you'd be angry.'

'I am *angry*,' Jason sniffed. 'Tilly's . . . I don't want it to be over.'

'It's not over,' I said without a pause.

Jason stopped crying for a second. 'What?'

I shrugged. 'It's not over between you and Tilly.'

A great trunk of an arm came across Jason's face and wiped, from elbow to wrist. 'It's not?'

I sat back, and tried to contain a smirk. 'Is that what you're getting so worked up over?'

'But . . .' Jason said. 'You and her . . .'

I sighed. 'Jason, I promise you that there is no me and Tilly.'

'Tilly and I,' Jason corrected. 'Tilly and I.'

I raised a finger of protest, stammered, then

retracted. Best not argue with the guy a hundred kilos bigger than me. 'Either way . . . Tilly's not cheating on you. I know this may not help, but . . . After that night . . . Tilly chose you.'

Jason blinked. 'But . . . she was *with* you.'

'A mistake,' I said, then bit my lip. 'That doesn't help either, does it?'

'Not really, no,' Jason said and shook his head.

'Fine.' I raised my hands and drummed the table. I was mucking up what I wanted to say. I wanted to say: *Hey, don't worry, things only seem shit*, without coming across as a complete know-it-all guru bastard. How do I say it? How do I put it into words? How do I make him feel better?

'If Tilly chose me . . .' Jason said. 'Why didn't she tell me about the baby?'

Great, now another question I don't know the answer to. Thanks a lot, Jason.

'Do you think . . .' Jason went on. 'She was scared?'

Yes, good, great angle, Jason – roll with that.

'I don't know,' Jason wiped his eyes. 'I . . . I am. I'm scared.'

'Of what?' I said.

'She didn't tell me,' Jason said. 'Which means . . .

I don't know, she doesn't trust me? I'm afraid she doesn't trust me.'

'Or,' I said, 'she's afraid you might leave.'

'I wouldn't leave,' Jason said.

That moment, more footsteps came toward me from the side. I heard clattering dishes, and I sniffed something sweet. Khirstyn appeared to my side with a bit of a smile and a cup of steaming tea. 'Here you go,' she said, placing the tea in front of me. 'You came a bit early – can't hook you up with a freebie yet.'

I shrugged. 'Maybe next time, huh?'

Khirstyn grinned. 'Sure. Next time.' She backed away from the table, and retreated behind the counter. I heard giggling. Were they making fun of me? I shook my head. Not important – Jason was my concern right now.

'Yes, I know, I know you wouldn't, Jason,' I said. 'It's only . . . People tend to run from their problems. They get scared, and they don't face them, you know?'

Jason frowned. 'But I could help her?'

I sighed. 'Maybe you were, and you just didn't know it.'

'What's that supposed to mean?'

'Well,' I said and took a long, deep, composing breath, 'maybe it was enough for you to be there. To listen, to help, if she'd asked you to. Maybe that's what

Tilly wanted from you.'

'To be there?' Jason said.

I nodded. 'Sometimes it's enough.'

Jason scoffed, sniffed again, and then scowled at the table. 'I deserved to know, though.'

'I think so too,' I said.

'So why didn't she?' Jason said. 'Why did she keep this from me?'

I looked around the room, trying to think of an answer. From the empty tea cups to the freshly set tables, I saw nothing. The rain trickled down the windows, the droplets glowing gold from the headlights of the traffic outside. One car turned into the car-park. I recognised it – sure enough, Mum clambered out from the driver's side.

And from the passenger's side, Tilly emerged.

'I don't have an answer to that, Jason.' I turned back to him, and nodded outside. 'But I know who would.'

Jason glanced outside, shivered and sniffed until there was nothing to sniff. He rubbed his eyes, frowned and looked up at me. 'I don't think I'm ready, Clem.'

'You know, Jason,' I said. 'I don't know if there is such a thing.'

Clem

Many months later . . .

I know, I know – seriously, Clem? *A time-skip?* Yes, yes, horrible, awful, how dare I! But here's the thing: the whole point of all this was to get ready. To be prepared when life came up and reared its ugly head. But here's the kicker. You see, life isn't a bitch: It's not some slobbering, monstrous mutt you have to avoid at all costs. No, life's more like a cat. A bastard of a cat, sure, but a cat all the same. Sometimes it curls in your lap and you think you can watch your damn show in peace, and sometimes it flips its shit for no reason, and you're left wondering where it all went wrong.

Before I get into that, I should probably sum up some things.

Firstly, Jason didn't beat me up. That was nice. Bullet, or rather fisticuffs, dodged. Instead, Jason went off with Tilly and had a real long discussion about what I can only assume was an even more awkward topic of conversation than I have ever had. That's a lesson there: Some people have it worse than me. Boom. Jason and Tilly had some turbulent times after that, then they broke up, and now they're sort of . . . I don't know if there's a term for it. *Mutually-unavailable-for-anybody-including-each-other*, is about as good a title as I've got. It's not the best . . . it's not the worst.

I find that oddly comforting.

Secondly, I asked Kihrstyn out. Now, now, now before you rattle off about how that's a 'typical male waitress fantasy' and how 'I shouldn't flirt with someone who is just working' you'll be very pleased to know I didn't flirt with her in the cafe.

It was at DRD. She came in one day . . . and another . . . and another, and then one day, when I finished, we awkwardly did the step-around sorry-swap.

'Sorry,' I said, stepping one way.

'Sorry,' she said, stepping the same way.

'Oh, sorry,' I said, stepping the other way.

'Sorry,' she said, smiled, then said. 'You come by the cafe sometimes, right?'

There was some talking, many forced jokes, fewer laughs, and one plonker of a baby-brag followed by a smooth transition into: 'I just thought I should be honest about something like that before . . . I mean, *if* we were to. . .'

Yeah, so she said no. And when she said it, I felt a great swell of relief. I don't know why, but I felt . . .

okay. I was fine, you know? There was nothing to worry about.

Lastly, the baby rocketed from nowhere. I wish there were a better way to phrase that. I've only been talking and panicking and stressing about this kid for the past nine months, but when it . . . *popped* out, shall we say, it happened rather quickly. A week before the baby was due, on a lazy, hazy afternoon, I got a call from Tilly to say she was having contractions.

'*Clem*,' she said. '*My water broke.*'

'Really?' I said. 'Hey! You're in the fifteen percent.'

'*Clem*!'

'Right,' I said. 'I uh . . . better put some shoes on.'

A couple of hours later, and there we were.

I've spent the last nine months practicing, building, studying to become an adult, and the one thing I've learned is that there is no hard and fast rule. I think . . . look, here's what I think I might have picked up here: it's not about material things – debts, loans, fees, bills, hell, it's not even about the things they get you, like houses and cars and flat-screen TVs. It's about how you deal with it all, whether that means preparing for it, or letting it happen. Sometimes it means facing your problems head on, sometimes it means stepping aside. I think after everything that's happened, I have nothing, or at least, no more than I did than when it all began, but *I* am more. I've learned that adulthood and maturity aren't the same thing; that adulthood is static, while maturity comes and goes. The real trick is to let it go when the times are good and grasp hold of it when the going gets rough.

Maybe you know what I mean. Maybe you don't. And that's fine, too, who am I to say otherwise? I'm no authority on anything, really. Just another *schmuck* trying to make sense of it all. But I think I've got it. I'm pretty sure I've got it . . . So here it is: I am twenty-one, and I am ready for my daughter.

Acknowledgements:

It's both surreal and extremely humbling to have the pleasure of thanking people for their support in helping me achieve my dream. This itty-bitty little slice of a story you hold in your hands was only possible because of these people.

Firstly, I would love to thank my family. Mum, for her stout belief that I would reach my goals. Dad, for his belief in writing for what I enjoy, and not for what others might. Ben, Sam, and Matt, my brothers, for enduring my endless brattle about the nitty-gritty of stories.

Secondly, to my friends, Adam, Declan, and Kyle, a surprisingly talented spread of misfits, and an endearingly supportive bunch of young men.

And thirdly, to *Scribendi,* and in particular, EM292 (I wish I could thank you by name), for understanding and improving the roughest of rough drafts.

Also to the rest of my friends and family —you are too many to list all in this *teeny-weeny* book (unless I stretch this baby out to a hundred pages) so I will say this: you know who you all are, and more importantly, you know how much I love you. Thank you all! If I've forgotten anybody, I'll thank you in the next book.

Cheers,

Luke

Luke Weavell is a writer from the Eastern Suburbs of Melbourne, Victoria. He runs a blog and youtube channel through his website, **www.lukeweavellwrites.com**, where he posts bi-weekly. '*Boy-Man*' is his first ever publication, and he hopes you enjoyed it.

www.ingramcontent.com/pod-product-compliance
Lightning Source LLC
Chambersburg PA
CBHW070530130626
46555CB00003B/1347